KU-622-477

Enid Blyton

A WISHING-CHAIR
ADVENTURE

A DARING
SCHOOL RESCUE

For Romilly and Perdy
A. P.

HODDER CHILDREN'S BOOKS
Text first published in Great Britain as chapters 10-14 of *The Wishing-Chair Again* in 1950
First published as *A Daring School Rescue: A Wishing-Chair Adventure* in 2019
by Egmont UK Limited
This edition published in 2021 by Hodder & Stoughton Limited

1 3 5 7 9 10 8 6 4 2

Enid Blyton ® and Enid Blyton's signature are registered trade marks of Hodder & Stoughton Limited
Text © 2021 Hodder & Stoughton Limited
Cover and interior illustrations by Alex Paterson. Illustrations © 2021 Hodder & Stoughton Limited

No trade mark or copyrighted material may be reproduced without the express written
permission of the trade mark and copyright owner.
The moral right of the author has been asserted.

All characters and events in this publication, other than those clearly
in the public domain, are fictitious and any resemblance to
real persons, living or dead, is purely coincidental.

All rights reserved.
No part of this publication may be reproduced, stored in
a retrieval system, or transmitted, in any form or by any means, without
the prior permission in writing of the publisher, nor be otherwise circulated
in any form of binding or cover other than that in which it is published
and without a similar condition including this condition being
imposed on the subsequent purchaser.

A CIP catalogue record for this book is available from the British Library.

ISBN 978 1 444 96000 6

Printed and bound in China

The paper and board used in this book are made from wood from responsible sources.

Hodder Children's Books
An imprint of
Hachette Children's Group
Part of Hodder & Stoughton
Carmelite House
50 Victoria Embankment
London EC4Y 0DZ

An Hachette UK Company
www.hachette.co.uk
www.hachettechildrens.co.uk

Enid Blyton

A WISHING-CHAIR
ADVENTURE

A DARING
SCHOOL RESCUE

X081441

**The item should be returned or renewed
by the last date stamped below.**

Dylid dychwelyd neu adnewyddu'r eitem erbyn
y dyddiad olaf sydd wedi'i stampio isod.

26 APR 2022

23 AUG 2023

- 8 DEC 2023

Tredegar House
Library

To renew visit / Adnewyddwch ar
www.newport.gov.uk/libraries

THE WISHING-CHAIR what magical adventure will it take the children on next?

The playroom at the bottom of the garden is where nearly all the wishing-chair's adventures begin . . .

PETER

MOLLIE

BINKY is the most helpful pixie you ever did meet

CHAPTER ONE
OFF TO FIND THE TOYS

Peter and Mollie got to the playroom door just as Binky was flying out in the wishing-chair.

Binky pulled them up with him. Then the chair flapped its **green and yellow wings** and flew strongly up into the air.

'Where are we going?' asked Mollie.

'I don't know,' said Binky. 'I just said to the chair, "Go and find Rosebud, and the rest of the **lost toys**," and it seemed to know the place I meant, because it rose up at once. I've no idea where we shall land. I only hope it's somewhere nice. It would be awful to go to the Village of Slipperies, or to the Land of Rubbish, or somewhere like that.'

'Oh dear – I hope it's somewhere nice, too,' said Mollie. 'The chair is flying very high, isn't it?'

'Do you think it may be going to **Toyland?**' asked Peter. 'I wouldn't mind that at all. I think it's very likely the toys may have gone there.'

'It certainly seems to be taking the way to Toyland as far as I remember,' said Binky, peering down. 'I know we pass over the

Village of Teddy Bears before we reach Toyland, and we're very near that now. There's Toyland, far over there. That must be where we're going.'

3

But it wasn't. The chair suddenly began to fly down and down at a great rate, and it was plain that it was going to land.

'Well! This isn't Toyland!' said Binky in surprise. 'Good gracious! I do believe it's the school run by Mister Grim, for **Bad Brownies**. Surely the toys haven't gone there!'

The chair landed in the grounds of a big house, just near a wall. Binky and the children got off. They pushed the chair under a bush to hide it. Then they looked cautiously round.

From the big building in the distance came
a **chanting noise.** The children and Binky
listened.

'I mustn't scream or whistle or shout
Because Mister Grim is always about,
I mustn't stamp or slam any door
Or jump or slide on the schoolroom floor,
I mustn't be greedy, untidy or lazy
Because Mister Grim would be driven quite CRAZY!'

'Ooooh!' said Mollie. 'I don't like the sound of that. That must be the poor Bad Brownie learning verses for **Mr. Grim**.'

'Yes,' said Binky. 'I do wish we hadn't come here. I've half a mind to get in the wishing-chair and go off again. I've always been told that Mister Grim is a very hard master. We don't want to be caught by him.'

'**Caught!**' said Peter. 'But we're two children and a pixie – we're not brownies – and this is a school for brownies.'

'I know,' said Binky. 'I just don't like the feel of this place, that's all. If you think it's all right, we'll stay and see if we can **possibly** find where our toys are.'

'I think we'd better,' said Peter. 'Well – what's the first thing to do?'

'Listen – is that the brownies coming out to play?' said Mollie as a perfect babel of noise reached them. Then came the sound of feet running and in a trice about fifty small brownies surrounded them. They all looked **merry, mischievous little fellows**, too young to have grown their brownie beards yet.

'Who are you? Are you new pupils for this awful school?' asked a small brownie, pushing himself forward. 'My name's **Winks**. What's yours?'

All the little brownies crowded round, listening eagerly. Binky pushed them back.

'Don't crowd so. No, we haven't come to your school. We came because we're looking for things we've **lost**, and we think they may be somewhere here. My name's Binky. These are real children, Peter and Mollie.'

'Well, be careful Mister Grim doesn't see you,' said Winks. 'He's in a **very bad temper** these days – worse than he's ever been.'

'What are you looking for?' asked another brownie. 'I'm Hoho; you can trust me.'

'Well,' said Binky, 'we came here to look for a lot of flying toys.'

'**Flying toys**!' said Winks. 'Well! Have we seen anything like that, boys?'

'Yes!' shouted Hoho at once. 'Don't you remember? Yesterday evening we saw something very peculiar – we thought they were curious birds flying about in the air. They must have been your toys.'

'What happened to them?' asked Peter.

'Well, old Grim was out in the garden,' said Hoho. 'And he suddenly looked up and saw them, too. He was very excited, and called out some words we couldn't hear . . .'

'And what we thought were the peculiar birds came right down to him,' said Winks.

'Well, whatever can he do with them?' said Hoho. 'We are never allowed any toys at all. I suppose he will sell them to his friend the **Magician Sly-Boots**.'

'Oh dear,' said Mollie. 'Well, we must try and get them before he does. Will you show us where you think Mister Grim might have hidden our toys?'

'Yes, we'll show you!' shouted the brownies. 'But do **be careful** you aren't caught!'

They took Binky and the children to the big

building, all walking on tiptoe and shushing each other.

Hoho led them inside. He pointed to a **winding** stair. 'Go up there,' he whispered. 'You'll come to a little landing. On the left side is a door. That's the storeroom, where I expect Mister Grim has put the toys.'

'Creep in – and see if you can find them,' whispered Winks.

'Come on,' said Binky to the others. 'It's now or never! If we find our things we'll take them and **rush** down and out into the garden,

and be off in the wishing-chair before Mister
Grim even knows we're here!'

'Sh!' said Mollie, and they all began to go up
the stairs on tiptoe. '**Shhhhhh!**'

CHAPTER TWO
MISTER GRIM'S SCHOOL FOR BAD BROWNIES

Up the stairs went the three, treading very quietly indeed, hoping that not one of the stairs would **creak** or **crack**.

The brownies crowded round the door at the bottom of the stairs, holding their breath and watching. Up and up and up – and there was the landing at last! Now for the door on the left.

They saw the door. They tiptoed to it and Peter turned the handle. Would it be **locked?** No, it wasn't!

They **peeped** inside. Yes, it was the storeroom, and stacks of books, pencils, rulers, ink-bottles, old desks, and all kinds of things were there.

'Can't see our toys,' whispered Binky. 'Let's look in all the drawers and all the cupboards.'

So they began opening the drawers and hunting in them, and pulling open the cupboard doors and peering in at the shelves. But they could find nothing more exciting than **books** and **pens** and **rubbers**.

And then Binky gave a soft cry. 'Look here,' he said. 'Here they are!'

The others ran quickly over to him. He had opened a **big chest** – and there, lying quietly in the top of it, their wings vanished, lay all the toys they had lost – yes, Rosebud was there, and Peter's engine, and the top and the soldiers – everything.

Then the children heard a noise that froze them to the floor. Footsteps – footsteps coming slowly and heavily up the stairs. Not light, quick, brownie steps, but slow, ponderous ones. Would the footsteps come to the storeroom?

In panic the children and Binky **squeezed** themselves into a cupboard, not having time to put away the toys they had pulled out of the chest. The door opened – and somebody walked in!

The children hardly dared to breathe and Binky almost choked. Then a voice spoke.

'**SOMEONE** has been here. **SOMEONE** has tried to steal toys. And that **SOMEONE** is here still. Come out!'

The children didn't move. They were much too scared to do a thing. And then poor Binky choked! He choked again, then coughed loudly.

Footsteps marched to the cupboard and the door was **flung** wide open.

There stood Mister Grim — exactly like his name! He was a big, burly brownie, with a tremendous beard falling to the floor. He had pointed ears and shaggy eyebrows that almost hid his eyes.

'**HO**!' he said in a booming voice. 'So the **SOMEONE** is not one person, but three!'

Peter, Mollie and Binky came out, poor Binky still coughing. Mister Grim took them each firmly by the back of the neck and sat them down on the window-seat.

'And now will you kindly tell me why you came to steal my toys?' he said.

'They're not your toys, sir,' Peter said at last in rather a trembling voice. 'They're ours. We let them grow wings yesterday by using **Growing Ointment** on them – and they flew away. We came to fetch them.'

'A very likely story indeed,' said Mister Grim scornfully. 'And how did you come here?'

'Up the stairs,' said Mollie.

Mister Grim frowned a fierce frown. 'Don't

be foolish, girl,' he said. 'I mean, how did you arrive here – by **bus** or **train** – and how did you get into the grounds?'

Binky gave the others a sharp nudge. Mollie had just been going to say that they had come in their wishing-chair, but she shut her mouth again tightly. Of course she mustn't give that away! Why, Mister Grim would search the grounds and find it!

'Well?' said Mister Grim. 'I am asking you a question – and when I ask questions I expect them to be answered.'

They didn't say a word. Mister Grim got up and put the toys back in the chest. 'You,' he said to Binky, 'you are a pixie, and I don't usually take pixies into my school. But you are a **very bad pixie**, I can see, and I shall keep you here. And I shall keep these two as well.

They deserve to be punished by being my pupils here for a term.'

'Oh, no!' said Mollie in horror. 'What will our mother say? You can't do that.'

'You will see,' said Mister Grim. 'Now go downstairs, find the brownie called Winks, and tell him you are to come into class when the bell rings. He will give you **books** and **pencils** and tell you where to sit.'

The three of them had to go downstairs in a row, Mister Grim behind them. They were frightened!

Unless they could manage somehow to get to their wishing-chair, they would simply *have* to stay at Mister Grim's school!

They found Winks and told him quickly what had happened. He was very sorry. '**Bad luck!**' he said. 'Very bad luck. Come on – I'll get you your books and things. Sit by me in class and I'll try and help you all I can.'

He took them into a big room and gave them books and pencils. Almost at once a bell rang **loudly** and all the brownies trooped in quickly. Not one of them spoke a word. They took their places quietly and waited.

'Why were you sent here, Winks?' whispered Binky as they all waited for Mister Grim to appear.

'Because I used my grandmother's **Blue Spell** and turned all her pigs blue,' whispered back Winks.

'And I was sent here because I put a spell into my father's shoe-tongues and they were **rude** to him all the way down our street and back,' whispered Hoho.

'And I was sent because . . .' began another brownie, when slow and heavy footsteps were heard. In came Mister Grim and stood at his big desk.

'Sit!' he said, as if the brownies were all little dogs. They sat.

'We have three new pupils,' said Mister Grim. 'I regret to say that I caught them stealing – **STEALING** – from my storeroom. Brrrrrr!'

This was very frightening. Mollie didn't

even dare to cry. She comforted herself by thinking of the wishing-chair **hidden** under the bush in the garden. They would run to it as soon as ever they could!

'Now we will have mental numbers,' said Mister Grim, and a little groan ran round the class. 'You, boy, what number is left when you take eighty-two and sixty-four from one hundred and three?'

He was pointing at poor Peter. Peter went **red**.

'Say six hundred and fifty,' whispered Winks. 'He doesn't know the answer himself!'

'Six hundred and fifty,' said Peter boldly. Everyone **clapped** as if he were right.

'Er – very good,' said Mister Grim. Then he pointed to Mollie. 'How many pips are there in seven pounds of raspberry jam?'

'**Seven pounds of raspberry jam?**' repeated Mollie, wondering if she had heard aright. 'Er – well . . .'

'Say none at all, because your mother only makes raspberry jelly and strains the pips out,' whispered Winks.

'Er – none at all,' said Mollie.

'How do you make that out?' thundered Mister Grim in a very frightening voice.

'Because my mother makes raspberry jelly and strains all the pips out,' said Mollie. Everyone clapped again.

'**Silence**!' said Mister Grim. 'Now you, pixie

– and see you are very, **very careful** in your answer. If I take fifty-two hairs from my beard, how many will there be left?'

Binky stared desperately at the long beard that swept down to the floor. 'Well,' he began . . . and then Winks whispered to him.

'Say "the rest"!' he hissed.

'Er – well, the rest of the hair will be left,' he said.

Mister Grim suddenly pounded on the desk with his hand. 'You, Winks!' he shouted. 'I heard you whispering then – you told him the answer – **you just wait**.'

CHAPTER THREE
BINKY IS NAUGHTY

Morning school came to an end at last. Mister Grim rapped on his desk.

'Attention, all of you!' he said. 'Dinner will be in ten minutes' time. Anyone who is late or who has **dirty hands** or **untidy hair** will go without.'

Winks groaned. 'It's awful,' he said to Peter when Mister Grim had gone out. 'There's never enough dinner for everyone, so Mister Grim just says, "Here, you, your hair is untidy," or "Here, you, your nails aren't clean," and about a dozen of us have to go **without our dinner**.'

'What a dreadful school! 'said Peter. 'Why don't you run away?'

'How can we?' said Winks. 'You've seen the high wall round the grounds, and all the gates are locked. I wish I could get out of here; it's a **horrid place**, and I really would be good if I could escape.'

'Would there be room for him in the wishing-chair, do you think?' whispered Mollie to Binky. 'He's **so nice**. I'd like to help him, Binky.'

'So would I,' whispered back Binky. 'Well, we'll see.'

Mister Grim stood at the door of the dining-

hall as each brownie walked in. Every so often he pounced on one and **roared** at him.

'Here, you, you haven't washed behind your ears! No dinner! Here, you, why aren't your nails scrubbed? No dinner!' And when Binky tried to slip past him he roared: 'Here, you, why haven't you brushed your hair? **No dinner**!'

'I did brush it,' said Binky indignantly, 'but

it's the kind of hair that won't lie down.'

'No dinner today for untidy hair, and no dinner tomorrow for answering back,' said Mister Grim.

'**Oh, I say,** that's not fair,' said Binky.

There was a little time before afternoon

school. Peter, Binky, Mollie and Winks had a meeting in a far corner of the grounds.

'Now listen,' said Winks. 'What about a bit of **magic** to get yourselves free?'

'Oooh, yes,' said Binky, looking very cheerful. 'That's an awfully good idea of yours, Winks. I'd forgotten about my **wand**. I'll be very naughty – and then we'll see what happens.'

They all went in to afternoon school feeling rather excited. What would happen? It would certainly be fun to see Binky being very **naughty!**

Mister Grim began firing questions at the class. 'Hands up those who know why brownies have long beards. Hands up those who know the magic word for "disappear". Hands up those who know why green smoke always comes out of chimneys of witches' houses. **Hands up** . . .'

He didn't even wait for anyone to answer so the brownies just shot up their hands at each question and then put them down again and waited for the next. Peter and Mollie thought it was the **silliest** class they had ever attended!

'And now – can anyone ask me a question

I can't answer?' said Mister Grim. 'Be careful –
because if I can answer it, you'll have to come
up and be punished.'

The brownies had all been caught by this
trick before, so nobody put up his hand.

'I've got a question; I've got a question!'
suddenly called out Binky, seeing a chance to
use his wand.

'What is it?' said Mister Grim, frowning.

'Mister Grim, why do horses wear hooves
instead of feet?' cried Binky.

'Come up here,' said Mister Grim sternly.
'That's another **silly question**.'

Binky went. 'Ha!' he shouted in delight. 'I've
got my lovely wand!'

Mister Grim snatched at it, but Binky was
skipping down the room, waving it.

'I'll give you all a **half-holiday!** Yes, I will!

See my wand waving to give you all a half-holiday! Go into the garden and play, all of you!'

The brownies didn't wait. They rushed out of the room at top speed, shouting and **laughing**. Soon only Peter, Mollie and Binky were left with Mister Grim. Winks was peeping round the door.

'How **DARE** you treat me like this!' shouted Mister Grim, marching towards Binky. 'I'll – '

'Go back, go back!' chanted Binky, and waved his wand at Mister Grim, whose feet at once took him six steps backwards, much to his surprise. 'Aha! I may have **powerful** magic, Mister Grim, so be careful!'

'Come on, Binky,' whispered Peter. 'Let's go and find the wishing-chair and **fly off**.'

'But I want my doll Rosebud before we go,' said Mollie. 'And have you forgotten your engine and all the other toys, Peter? We must take those with us. Mister Grim, give us our toys!'

'Certainly not,' said Mister Grim, and he shook a large key at them. 'See this key? It's the key of the storeroom, which I've **locked**. You can't get your toys and you never shall!'

CHAPTER FOUR
HOME, WISHING-CHAIR, HOME!

'I think we'd better go,' Binky said in a low voice to Peter and Mollie.

They **darted** out of the door and Mister Grim followed. But just outside the door he ran into a crowd of brownies that popped up from nowhere quite suddenly, and over he went! When he got up the children and Binky were **nowhere** to be seen.

Binky and the others **raced** to find the wishing-chair. Where was the bush they had hidden it in? Ah, there it was! They ran to the bush – but, oh dear, the chair wasn't there!

'One of the brownies must have found it and taken it,' said Binky. Just then Winks ran up and pulled at his arm.

'I found your wishing-chair and hid it in the shed,' he said. 'I was afraid Mister Grim might see it if he walked round the garden. Come along – I'll show you where it is.' He took the three to an old broken-down shed. The roof had fallen in at one end. There were no windows to the shed, so it was very **dark** inside. Binky groped his way in – and immediately fell over the wishing-chair.

The wings waved gently as they felt Binky's anxious hands. The chair **creaked** softly. Binky knew it was glad to have him again.

'Wishing-chair, we must go quickly,' said Binky, and he climbed on to the seat. 'Come on, Peter and Mollie – quickly, before Mister Grim comes!'

'What about Winks? Aren't we going to take him, too?' said Mollie.

'Oh – would you really?' said Winks, in **delight**. 'You really are very kind. I hate this school. I've been trying to escape for ages.'

He was just about to squeeze in the chair with the others when somebody appeared at the doorway. It was Mister Grim!

'So here you are!' he said, peering in.

'Fly out where the roof has fallen in, fly out there!' suddenly shouted Winks. 'The chair can just squeeze through it!'

And the chair rose up into the air and flew to where the roof had fallen in! It got **stuck** half-way through, but Peter broke away a bit more roof and the chair suddenly shot through and out into the open air.

'Oh, poor Winks – we've left him there,'
cried Mollie, almost in tears.

'Go on, chair, **fly off with them!**' shouted
Winks from below in the shed. 'Don't mind
me! Escape while you can.' The chair flew out
of hearing. Binky and Peter were very silent.
Mollie wiped her eyes with her hanky.

'We'll go back for him,' said Binky, taking
Mollie's hand.

'And what about our toys, too?' said Mollie, with a sniff. 'It's **dreadful** to have to leave Rosebud behind, too.'

'And my engine,' said Peter, gloomily, 'and the skittles and soldiers.'

'We'll get them all back,' said Binky, comfortingly. 'You wait and see.'

The chair took them back to the playroom. It gave a creaking sort of sigh and set itself down in its place. Its wings at once vanished.

'There! Its wings have gone already,' said Mollie, ready to cry again. 'So now we can't go and rescue Winks today.'

Mother's voice was heard calling down the garden. 'Children! It's past **tea-time** – and you didn't come in to dinner either. Where are you?'

'Oh, dear – now we shall have to go,' said

Mollie. 'And we haven't planned anything. Binky, come and tell us **AT ONCE** if the chair grows its wings again – and do, do try to think of a good plan.'

'Come and see me again tonight if you can,' called Binky. 'I may have a visitor here who will help us.'

After supper they **slipped down** to the playroom. Binky wasn't there. There was a note left on the table, though.

Gone to have supper with Tickles.
Felt very hungry after having no dinner.
Be back later. Can you come and meet my
visitor at half-past nine if you're not asleep?
VERY IMPORTANT.
Love from Binky

'I know, Peter,' said Mollie, 'let's go to bed now, then we can slip out for half an hour and meet Binky's visitor without feeling guilty. We simply must meet him if it's **important**.'

Both children went to sleep – but Peter awoke at half-past nine because he had set the alarm clock for that time and put it under his pillow. When the alarm went off, muffled by the pillow, he awoke at once. He slipped on his dressing-gown and went to wake Mollie.

'Come on!' he whispered. 'It's half-past nine. **Buck up!**' Mollie put on her dressing-gown, too, and the two of them slipped out of the garden door and down to the playroom. They peeped in at the door. Yes – Binky's visitor was there – but, dear me, what a very, very **surprising** one!

CHAPTER FIVE
MISTER CUBB'S STRANGE ARMY

Binky saw the children peeping in. He got up from the sofa and called them. 'Hallo! I'm so glad you've come. Come along in. I've got an old friend here, and I want you to meet him.'

The old friend stood up – and what do you think he was? He was a tall **teddy bear**, so old that his hair had turned grey! He was not as tall as they were, but a bit taller than Binky.

'This is Mister Cubbs, the ruler of Teddy Bear Village,' said Binky. The teddy bear bowed politely, and shook hands.

'I've been telling **Mister Cubbs** about your toys that Mister Grim has got, and won't give you back,' said Binky.

'I think Mister Grim should be forced to give them up to you,' said Mister Cubbs earnestly. 'I propose that I raise a **little army** from Toyland and march on the school.'

Peter and Mollie gazed at him in wonder and astonishment. It all sounded like a **dream** to them – but a very exciting and interesting

dream. An army from Toyland! Good gracious – whoever heard of such a thing?

'Mister Cubbs has very great influence in Toyland,' explained Binky. 'In fact, he has now ruled over it for nearly **a hundred years**.'

'Are you really a hundred years old!' asked Mollie, amazed.

'One hundred and fifty-three, to be exact,' said Mister Cubbs, with a polite little bow. 'Now, what I suggest is this. I will send to the wooden soldiers, the clockwork animals and the sailor dolls – and also my teddies, of course, and tell them to meet me at a certain place. They will make a very fine army.'

'And you'll **march on the school**, I suppose?' said Binky. 'And when you have defeated Mister Grim you will rescue Rosebud, the doll, and the other toys?'

'Exactly,' said Mister Cubbs.

'Can we come, too?' said Peter, excited. 'I'd **simply love** to see all this.'

'I'll send you word when we mean to march,' said the teddy bear. 'It will probably be tomorrow evening. Well, I must go now. Thank you for a very pleasant evening, Mister Binky.'

They went back to bed, hoping that the wishing-chair would grow its wings the next night if the teddy bear gathered together his curious little army.

They raced downstairs as soon as they could and were met by a very excited Binky.

'I'm so glad you've come. The wishing-chair has grown little buds of wings already – they'll sprout properly in a minute! And the teddy bear has sent to say that his army is on the **march!**'

'Oh – *what* a bit of luck!' cried the children, and ran to the chair. Just as they got to it the knoblike buds on its legs burst open – and out spread the **lovely green and yellow wings** again! They began to flap at once and made quite a wind.

'Come on,' said Peter, sitting in the chair. 'Let's go! And, Binky, don't let's forget to take Winks away from that horrid school, if we can. He can live with you here in the playroom if he hasn't got a home to go to.'

Mollie got in and Binky sat on the back of the chair.

Out of the door they flew at **top speed**.

The wishing-chair was told to go to Mister Grim's. 'But don't go down into the grounds,' commanded Binky. 'Just hover about somewhere so that we can see what's going on, and can dart down if we need to.'

It wasn't really very long before the chair was hovering over the front gate of Mister Grim's school. Not far off were all the brownies, marching up and down in the big school yard, doing drill with Mister Grim.

Then the marching brownies suddenly caught sight of the wishing-chair hovering in the air, and they set up a great shout.

'Look! They've come back! **Hurrah** for Binky and Peter and Mollie!'

Mister Grim stared up, too. He looked really furious, and, to the children's dismay, he bent down and picked up a big stone. It came **whizzing** through the air at them, but the wishing-chair did a little leap to one side and the stone passed harmlessly by.

Then Binky gave the others a nudge. 'Here comes the army! **DO** look!'

The children looked – and dear me, up the lane marched the strangest little army the children had ever imagined. First came the grey-haired teddy bear, swinging a little sword. Then came a row of wooden soldiers, **beating drums**. Then another row blowing trumpets. After them came a whole collection of clockwork animals.

'There's a jumping kangaroo!' cried Binky in glee. 'And a **dancing bear!**'

'And a running dog – and a walking **elephant!**' said Mollie in delight.

'And look — a pig that turns head-over-heels, and a duck that waddles!' shouted Peter, almost falling out of the chair in his excitement. 'And behind them all are the **sailor dolls**. Don't they look smart!'

The strange army came to the gate. The clockwork kangaroo jumped right over it to the other side. He undid the gate and opened it for the army to walk through.

The brownies saw the toys before Mister Grim did and shouted in joy. They ran to meet them. 'Who are you? Where have you come from?' they called. 'Can we **play with you?** We never have any toys here!

>'We've come for Mister Grim,
>We don't like Mister Grim,
>We've come to capture him,
>We've come for Mister Grim!'

chanted all the toys.

Mister Grim stared at them as if he couldn't believe his eyes. 'After him!' shouted the teddy bear, and after him they went! He turned to run – but the jumping kangaroo got between his legs and tripped him up, and there he was, **bumping** his nose on the ground, yelling for mercy!

The toys swarmed all over him in delight.

'Don't pull my hair! Don't cut off my **beautiful beard**,' begged Mister Grim. The teddy bear seemed just about to saw the long beard off with his sword! The children and Binky saw it all from their seat up in the wishing-chair and were just as **excited** as the toys and the brownies.

'I'll leave you your beard on one condition,' said the teddy bear, solemnly. 'Go and get the toys you have imprisoned here and bring them out to us.'

Mister Grim got up, looking very **frightened**, and went indoors.

He came out with all the toys. Mollie gave a scream of delight when she saw Rosebud.

The chair flew down to Mister Grim, and the children took all their toys from him. Mollie **cuddled** Rosebud happily.

'Thank you,' she said to the grey-haired teddy bear. 'You and your army have done very, very well. Do please bring any of them to see us whenever you can.'

The brownies crowded round the chair. 'Take us back with you, take us back.'

'We've only room for one of you, and that's Winks,' said Binky, firmly. 'Come on, Winks.'

Up got Winks, **grinning** all over his little brownie face. The wishing-chair rose up in the air. 'Goodbye, goodbye!' shouted Binky and the others. 'Let us know if Mister Grim behaves too badly to you and we'll send the army once again! **Goodbye!**'

Off they went, with all the toys and

brownies **waving** madly. Mister Grim didn't wave. He looked very down in the mouth indeed – but nobody was sorry for him, not even Mollie!

THE MAGIC FARAWAY TREE

The Land of
BIRTHDAYS

The Land of MAGIC
MEDICINES

The Land of
DO-AS-YOU-PLEASE

The Land of
TOYS

The Land of
ENCHANTMENTS

Collect all the magical Faraway Tree Adventures – packed full of exciting new colour illustrations!

The Land of GOODIES

In SANTA CLAUS'S CASTLE

The Land of DREAMS

The Land of SILLY SCHOOL

A WISHING-CHAIR
ADVENTURE

Discover more magical
Wishing-Chair adventures!

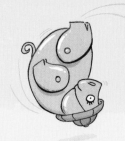